MARC BROWN

ARTHUR'S TEACHER TROUBLE

Little, Brown and Company

Boston   Toronto   London

**For Tucker Eliot Brown
A winner in my book every day!**

Library of Congress Cataloging-in-Publication Data

Brown, Marc Tolon.
   Arthur's Teacher Trouble.

   Summary: Third-grader Arthur is amazed when he is
chosen to be in the school spellathon.
   [1. Schools–Fiction.   2. Teachers–Fiction.
3. Animals–Fiction] I. Title.
PZ7.B81618Am   1986   [E]   86-3539
ISBN 0-316-11244-5
ISBN 0-316-11186-4 (pbk.)

HC: 10 9 8 7 6 5 4
PB: 10 9 8 7 6

                  WOR

*Joy Street Books are published
by Little, Brown and Company (Inc.)*

*Published simultaneously in Canada
by Little, Brown & Company (Canada) Limited*

Printed in the United States of America

The bell rang.

The first day of school was over.

Kids ran out of every classroom—every one but Room 13.

Here, the students filed out slowly, in alphabetical order.

"See you tomorrow," said their teacher, Mr. Ratburn.

"I can't believe he gave us homework the first day," said Arthur.
"I had the Rat last year," said Prunella. "Boy, do I feel sorry for you!"

"Make one wrong move," warned Binky Barnes, "and he puts you on death row."

"He's really a vampire with magical powers," said Chris.

As everyone was leaving, the principal came out of his office. "Are you ready for the September spellathon?" he asked.

"Yes!" cheered the crowd.

"Who's going to win this year?" asked the principal.

"Me!" everyone shouted.

"If I win again this year, do I get my name on the trophy twice?" asked Prunella.

"Not if I can help it," whispered Francine.

When Arthur got home, he slammed the back door.
"How was school?" Mother asked.
"I got the strictest teacher in the whole world,"
grumbled Arthur.

"Have a chocolate chip cookie," said Mother.
"Don't have time," said Arthur. "I have tons of homework."
"I'll eat Arthur's," said D.W. "I don't have any homework."
"You don't even go to school," said Arthur.
"I know." D.W. smiled.

After dinner Arthur was still doing homework.

"What's that?" asked D.W.

"It's a map of Africa," said Arthur.

"Looks like a pepperoni pizza," said D.W. "Next year when I'm in kindergarten, I won't have *any* homework. Ms. Meeker never gives it."

"Mom!" called Arthur. "D.W.'s being a pest."

"Time for bed," said Mother. "You can finish your map of Florida in the morning."

"*Africa,*" said Arthur.

The next day, Mr. Ratburn announced a spelling
test for Friday. "I want you to study very hard,"
he said. "The test will have a hundred words."
Buster looked pale.

"And," continued Mr. Ratburn, "the two students with the highest scores will represent our class at the all-school spellathon."

That week everyone in Arthur's class studied harder than ever. Arthur spent a lot of time looking for quiet places to study.

Suddenly it was Friday and time for the test.
Arthur could smell Miss Sweetwater's class
making popcorn.
He could hear Mrs. Fink's class leaving for a trip
to the aquarium. "Why did *we* have to get stuck
with the Rat?" he whispered to Francine.

Mr. Ratburn corrected their papers during lunch. "Class," he said, "most of you did very well on the test. But only two of you spelled *every* word correctly."

Muffy smiled. Francine hiccupped.

Buster patted his good-luck charm.

Mr. Ratburn cleared his throat.

"Our class representatives for the spellathon will be the Brain and Arthur."

"There must be some mistake!" said Muffy.

Mr. Ratburn gave Arthur and the Brain each a special list of words. "Just study these and you'll be ready for the spellathon in two weeks," he said.

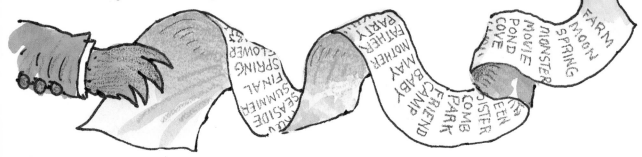

Arthur's family helped him study. Grandma asked Arthur his spelling words.

"How about your C-H-O-R-E-S?" Father asked. "Have you made your B-E-D?" Mother added.

D.W. helped, too. When Francine and Buster came over, D.W. answered the door. "Arthur can't play, but I can," she said. "I don't have to study."

"I can't believe the spellathon is finally here," said Grandma.
"Maybe now we'll get a little peace and quiet," D.W. said.
"Good luck, Arthur," said Mother and Father.

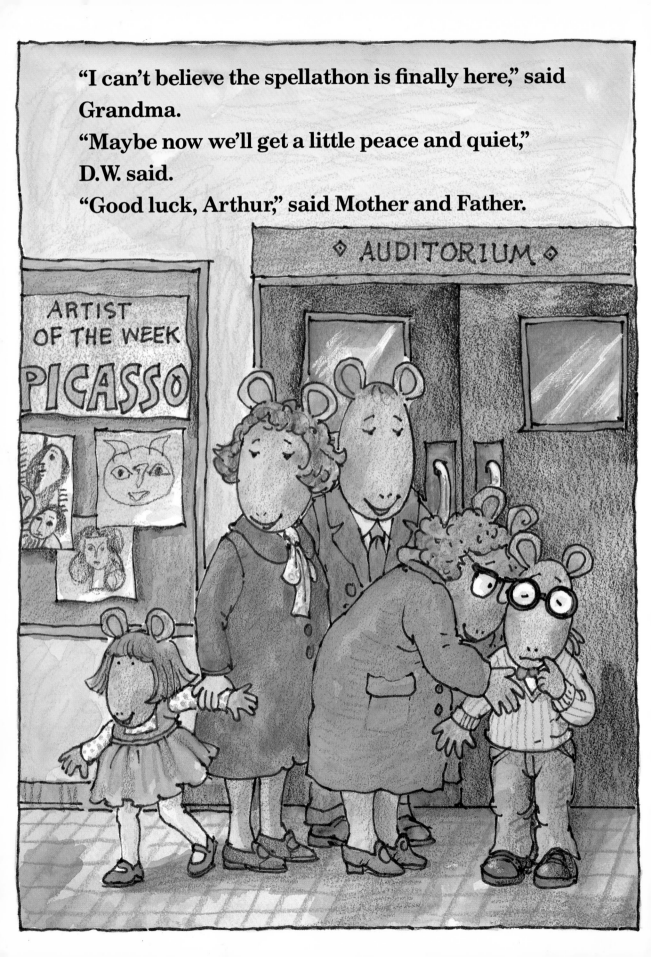

From backstage Arthur could hear the whole
school out in the auditorium.
"Well, today's the big day," said Mr. Ratburn.
"How do you feel?"
"I feel fine," the Brain answered.
Arthur gulped. "I wish I were still back in bed!"

The principal welcomed everyone and explained the rules.

The Brain had the first turn. He stepped up to the microphone.

"The first word is *fear*," said the principal.

"F-E-R-E," said the Brain, a little too quickly.

"I'm sorry," said the principal. "That's not correct."

"Are you sure?" asked the Brain.

"What dictionary are you using?"

The Brain wasn't the only one to drop out quickly.
The representatives from Miss Sweetwater's and
Mrs. Fink's class were gone in a flash.
Before long, only Arthur and Prunella were left.

It was Prunella's turn.

"The word is *preparation*," said the principal.

Prunella looked down at her feet.

"Could I have the definition, please?" she asked after a moment.

"Preparation," the principal repeated. "The process of getting ready."

"Of course," said Prunella. "P-R-E-P," she paused,

"E-R-A-T-I-O-N."

"I'm sorry, that's incorrect," said the principal.

"Now Arthur gets a chance to spell it."

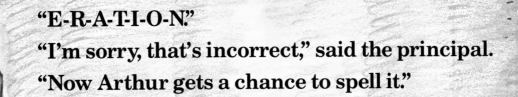

Arthur looked out over the audience and took a deep breath.

"Preparation," he said. "P-R-E-P-A-R-A-T-I-O-N."

"Correct!" said the principal.

Everyone in Mr. Ratburn's class cheered.

Then Mr. Ratburn went to the microphone. "I'm very proud of Arthur," he said. "In fact, I'm proud of my whole class. They worked very hard. This is the last third grade I'll have in the spellathon. But next year I look forward to a new challenge . . .